THE MONUMENT

OTHER YEARLING BOOKS BY GARY PAULSEN YOU WILL ENJOY:

THE SCHERNOFF DISCOVERIES

TUCKET'S RIDE

THE RIVER

THE WINTER ROOM

THE BOY WHO OWNED THE SCHOOL

THE COOKCAMP

THE VOYAGE OF THE *FROG*

HARRIS AND ME

A CHRISTMAS SONATA

MR. TUCKET

CALL ME FRANCIS TUCKET

THE CULPEPPER ADVENTURES SERIES

GARY PAULSEN WORLD OF ADVENTURE SERIES

YEARLING BOOKS are designed especially to entertain and enlighten young people. Patricia Reilly Giff, consultant to this series, received her bachelor's degree from Marymount College and a master's degree in history from St. John's University. She holds a Professional Diploma in Reading and a Doctorate of Humane Letters from Hofstra University. She was a teacher and reading consultant for many years, and is the author of numerous books for young readers.

Gary Paulsen

THE
MONUMENT

A Yearling Book

Published by
Dell Publishing
a division of
Bantam Doubleday Dell Publishing Group, Inc.
1540 Broadway
New York, New York 10036

ISBN: 0-440-40782-6

Reprinted by arrangement with Delacorte Press

Printed in the United States of America

August 1993

20   19   18   17   16

CWO

This book is dedicated in loving memory to my father, OSCAR PAULSEN, COL., UNITED STATES ARMY *(ret.),* *served 1928–1949,* *who should have had a monument.*

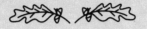

ROCKY

One

SOMETIMES it's funny how we can't know things. I get cranky about that, but I'm always getting that way about something or other, so it doesn't matter.

But it's still funny.

Like if Python hadn't killed the chicken he wouldn't have been sent to prison, and I wouldn't have helped him escape. He wouldn't have become my friend and led me to meet Mick so I could come to know all there is to know about art and life and sex and love and how Bolton, Kansas, is a microcosm of the world, even China, and I didn't know any of that was coming. Or even what the word *microcosm* meant until Mick told me, but that's what I mean.

Exactly. I couldn't know any of that was going to happen.

Mick says that life is wonderful that way. He says that life is really, *really* organic. It moves all the time and flexes when you least expect it to flex, which he likes, but I think sucks. I mean I want to know every little thing that's going to happen and not have any surprises. But I can't and that sometimes makes me mad.

Well, never mind. I got carried away.

Mick said I shouldn't get mad because it colors what I see and I won't be a good artist. I told him that I would maybe write down all of the things that happened and try to figure them out because I didn't like not knowing things. He said fine, do it, but don't get mad.

So I won't.

But it's hard.

Two

I DON'T KNOW my real name or even if I had one. When I was a baby my mother left me in the backseat of a police car in Kansas City, Kansas, and I don't remember name, place, what she was like—none of it.

I don't even know if it was true except that the sisters at Our Lady of Bleeding Redemption Orphanage told me that, and they aren't supposed to lie so maybe it's true.

They named me Rachael Ellen Turner, the sisters, but I got the nickname of Rocky because I threw rocks to make up for being small. I lived at Our Lady until I was nine years old, and I didn't think there was any way that I would be adopted.

I didn't have many friends because about the time you got to know somebody they would get adopted, and I didn't because of my color and my left leg.

Oh, they said it was for other reasons—there was always some excuse—but it was really my color and my left leg. I am the color of light caramel and have curly tight hair and even though they told us it didn't count, it was a fact that lighter-colored kids got adopted right away and the darker ones didn't. Along with that was my leg.

When I was born I guess my mother drank or smoked or did drugs or something, and my left leg didn't grow right. The sisters sent me to a doctor and they did some operations, but finally the doctors said all they could do was kind of fuse the knee so it wouldn't bend and let it grow straight and that's what happened. It grew with the rest of me and isn't too skinny or anything but I can't bend it, and so I've always walked kind of funny on it, and I get tired really easy, even now, when I'm thirteen and grown.

Every time somebody would come to look at little girls to adopt, I'd come walking into the conference room with those braces on my left leg and you could see the light go out in their eyes. I used to make small bets with myself as to how long it would take—ten, fifteen seconds. Never a minute on the big clock on the wall and the light was gone. The sisters used to help me get looking nice and do my hair so I would make a good first impression, a new dress and everything just so, but I knew it didn't matter.

Nobody wants a caramel kid with braces. Not from the start. Sometimes they'll love a kid if they already have one and they have to get braces, but not from the start.

So I didn't get adopted and didn't get adopted. I thought I might as well figure on staying at Our

Lady until I got pregnant and had to leave, like Mary Ferguson, and that would be my life.

Then came Emma and Fred.

Four days after my ninth birthday Sister Gene Autry—her real name was Sister Eugene but we saw an old cowboy movie on television once and she looked just like the cowboy who was named Gene Autry—came into my cubicle where I was reading a book about horses. I always wanted a horse and sometimes, when I was reading, I could think I owned a horse and it was nearly real. I drew pictures of horses from magazines, and sometimes I could almost think I was riding them. Well. Not really. But close.

"Quick, clean up!" Sister Gene Autry told me. "Hurry."

"Why?"

"They're back—the Hemesvedts are back. And they want to see you." She pulled at my hair. "Hurry. We want you to look good because . . . well, just because."

Because these people were the first ones to actually come back after seeing me with my leg brace, that was why, but I didn't say anything and let her comb my hair out and try to get me looking nice.

Mick said I was pretty—like a deer—because I've got big brown eyes and freckles across my nose and brown hair with just a little red in it, but I don't think so. You don't see really pretty women with one leg stiff. Even though he swore it didn't make any difference it did because it was in my head that way—that I couldn't be pretty with a bad leg.

But Sister Gene Autry fussed with me, her hands moving around my hair like small flying birds. She did the best she could, and we went out into the conference room, and there sat Emma and Fred Hemesvedt.

And of course I thought of the Flintstones right away, even though they didn't look at all like the Flintstones.

Fred was tall and thin except he had sort of a gut, and Emma was short and round, and they smiled a lot, at me and at each other and at Sister Gene Autry and Emma said:

"We decided we want to adopt you."

"You do?"

Sister Gene Autry pinched my arm so hard I almost squealed but I shut my mouth and stayed silent.

"Yes. We want you to join our family and come to live with us."

And that was how I came to live in Bolton, Kansas.

Three

WHEN I FIRST came to Bolton I wasn't sure that I wanted to be there no matter how nice Emma and Fred turned out to be.

It was a small town—I found later it had just two thousand people—and it seemed to be there just because it was too far from the last town to the next town.

There wasn't a reason to put a town where

Bolton was—not one. The country around Bolton is totally flat, flatter than even the rest of Kansas, and Mick says Kansas is the flattest place on earth.

So they put this little town here and there are farms all around it, and when we drove toward it in the car—Fred leaning back in the seat and telling me how much fun it would be—I almost asked them to go back.

I'd seen mountains on television and hills on television and saw some hills in Kansas City, and this wasn't right. There was nothing to stop your seeing. You just saw out and out until you couldn't see any farther.

But I remembered the last thing Sister Gene Autry said to me:

"Keep your mouth shut."

And so I did that and so I moved to Bolton with Emma and Fred and settled down to family life, except there wasn't any.

Somehow in all the interviews and examinations and tests and talking the state authorities and the sisters had not learned all the things there were to know about Emma and Fred.

That they drank.

Oh, they're nice enough and they have never, never done anything bad to me. Not even a loud word. They always let me do what I want, and even when I do something wrong they aren't bad about it. Fred just looks at me, smiles, and says:

"Let's do better next time." And Emma nods and pats me on the hand and says, "She will, she will, won't you, Rachael?"

But most of the time, all of the time, they drink. Fred owns the local grain elevator where the farmers come to sell their grain, and he keeps a bottle in his office, and Emma sits at home with a big gallon jug of red wine and watches the soaps, and they drink.

They don't fight. Fred always goes to work, except on the weekends when he watches sports on television, and Emma always takes care of the house. I think they love me and are very good to me and are completely drunk by nine o'clock every morning so that the world is just one long alcohol haze for them, but it isn't so bad.

Not as bad as the orphanage. Even with them

drinking and Emma and her soaps it isn't so bad.

Inside of a month I knew I had figured how to work around the drinking and spent most of my time alone, eating meals with them now and then and going on drives sometimes on Sunday morning before Fred got too drunk to drive, but other than that I just did things on my own.

Oh, there was school. There still is school. But school in Bolton was like school at the orphanage, except that the teachers don't hit you like the sisters do. I don't make friends really easy so at first I just kind of stayed by myself.

Then I met Traci and she became my best friend until Python, and we did lots of things together except that Traci liked to ride her bike, and I couldn't ride a bike very well because my left leg didn't bend.

But then Traci moved. Her father worked with the highway department and got transferred and she moved. I didn't get a new friend but it was still all right.

I met Python.

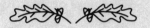

PYTHON

Four

IT WAS FUNNY how it happened. Even though it doesn't really have to do with Mick and the monument, it's part of how I came to live in Bolton the way I did so it's important.

Mick says Bolton is a microcosm of the world, and I looked it up and it means a smaller version of the rest of the world, and I guess he's right.

If you look at the center of Bolton there is the

city part, with Nicherson's grocery store where the sidewalks are cracked and all the ants come out of the cracks, and Hillary's hardware store and the dime store and two gas stations and three bars and two churches—just like a small big city.

Bolton is the county seat and so in the middle of the town there is a large grass area and an old courthouse with a flagpole and big old black cannon out front with a bunch of round balls welded in a pile. I know they're welded because I tried to get one loose and they didn't move. On the flagpole is the United States flag and just below it the Kansas flag, and every morning Sarah Widmerk, who is the court clerk, comes down the steps and raises the two flags and looks up at them in the morning light and then walks back up the stairs and goes to clerking.

Out around the middle part of town there are the houses where all the town people live, like Emma and Fred and me, and outside that there is another ring of houses where people who work for the other town people live, like Garret

Emerson, who works for Fred at the elevator and has about thirty-seven kids.

Out there, in that outer ring, most of the people don't have a lot of money so they have big gardens. Some of them keep goats and chickens and that was the problem.

Something about animals gets me. I don't know why, but maybe it's that we couldn't play with animals at the orphanage. So when I see an animal, a dog or cat or a horse or a goat or even a chicken, I want to touch it and play with it, and even now when I'm thirteen going on fifty—like Mick told me—I'm the same. I've just got to touch them.

But Emma and Fred can't have animals because Emma gets all swollen and bleeds out her nose from the animal hair, so I would sometimes go out to the outer ring of houses and pet goats and dogs and chickens, and one day out there I saw Python.

Of course he didn't have a name then.

He was just a big, scruffy dog with his ribs sticking out and curly tight hair all over his body, and you could tell he was starving. I hadn't seen

him around and don't know where he came
from. The first time I saw him I was standing in
front of the Seversons' yard, and there was a
loud noise from their chicken coop in back of the
house. When I ran around—Mrs. Severson came
out of the back door of the house with a baseball
bat at the same time—I saw this dog come bar-
reling out of the door of the coop with a chicken
in his mouth. He looked at me, then up at Mrs.
Severson with the bat, and took off. He cleared
the fence around the coop like he had wings,
and while he was flying he swallowed the
chicken.

Whole.

And that was how I came to name him. The
year before Emma and Fred had taken me to the
county fair. There was a side show with some
animals in it, and in one glass case they had a
big python.

"Ten feet long, big around as a man's leg and
alive—see it on the inside!" the man yelled. Fred
took me in while Emma tried to throw nickels
on some glass plates, although they kept sliding
off.

And it was all pretty tacky except that the snake was real, and in the case with the snake they had a chicken.

The chicken looked like it had been in there eight or nine years. It was half bald and walked around pecking at things, now and then pecking at the snake which lay back in a corner. I asked a man wearing dirty clothes and picking his nose what the chicken was for.

"Snake food," he said. "What did you think?"

Well it didn't look to me like the snake was ever going to move, let alone eat a chicken, and we turned to leave. Just then the snake's head came up, it flicked its tongue twice and whap, it nailed the chicken.

There were some feathers flying around, the chicken kicked once or twice, then the snake opened its jaws and swallowed the chicken.

Whole.

And that's how I named Python.

Except that I didn't see him again right away. He took the fence and was gone, chicken and all, in maybe two seconds. Mrs. Severson swore a little and went in to call the sheriff and I limped for home, and that was it.

Bolton doesn't have a dogcatcher. We have the county sheriff who is named Kelvin, Warren Kelvin, and the next morning when I got up I knew I was going to Kelvin's place.

It was impossible not to go. He had a pen out back, a chain-link concrete pen. That's where they kept the stray dogs until either somebody came to pick them up or Kelvin took them out and shot them, which is usually what happened. I had spent the whole night thinking of the dog flying over the fence and how it wouldn't be right for Kelvin to shoot him.

I got to the pen just after dawn, and sure enough, there was the dog.

He was sitting on the concrete, leaning against the fence. When I squatted next to him he growled, a low sound, but it wasn't mean and I knew it wasn't, and I put my hand through the fence and petted him and said:

"Hello, Python."

Five

IT REALLY happened that fast. When I knew his name and said it, he looked at me through the fence and stuck his muzzle down, scarred like it was a road map, and licked my fingers where they were on the wire. There wasn't anything I could do except break him out of there.

I waited until dark and came back and unlatched the gate and let him loose. I thought he would run but he didn't.

He came to me and stood next to me in the darkness and leaned so his shoulder was against my leg, his fur warm and the muscle tight under the skin. I petted him and thought he would leave then but he still didn't but stood, waiting. When I took a step, he took one, and when I stopped, he stopped.

It was like he was bolted to my leg, would only move when I moved. I grabbed the hair on the top of his shoulder, which about came to my waist, and leaned on him a bit to take the weight off my stiff leg. We started away from the pen and headed home, and never once after that did Python leave my side except when I went into a building.

He wouldn't come inside but stopped just outside the door and lay down when we got home that night. I told Emma and Fred what I had done and that I wanted to keep Python no matter what. I said that I would sleep outside in a special house with Python if I had to so he could live with us and Fred smiled.

"You don't have to worry, Rocky. I'll build him a house and he'll stay outside just fine. Emma doesn't mind, do you, Emma?"

And of course she didn't, just as they didn't mind anything I did that was half crazy, except that this time it wasn't. Half crazy.

Python turned out to be the best thing that ever happened to me next to Emma and Fred. The next morning Fred went to work and called the sheriff from work. When he came home that night he told me:

"Python is your dog now. I have cleared him with the law. You must take him for his shots and have Doc Emerson check him over, and I will make a doghouse for him Sunday."

And that's how Python came into my life and he has never left it since. When I go in the house, winter or summer, it doesn't matter, he stops at the door, has never once tried to get in. No matter how long or short I am in the house, when I come out he is by the door and stands up. I grab the hair on his shoulder and he walks with me. When I go to school or the movies or the library it's the same. He stops at the door and waits and everybody knows him and that he is my friend. Nobody, nobody touches him, or me when he's with me.

Except once.

There was a boy that lived here named Kyle Offens. Kyle was one of those people who tease other people who aren't right, and he took to teasing me because he thought my leg was funny. I didn't pay any attention because of what Kyle was like—he had a brain about the size of my little fingernail and only knew three words or maybe four—but one afternoon when I was walking past him on the way home from school, he started teasing me and took a poke at my arm. It wasn't much of a poke, and I didn't even notice it—just a touch.

But in about half a second he was on his back. Python had him down and was standing on his chest and had all his teeth showing. He was growling deep in his chest so that it sounded like a car engine inside a garbage can, and Kyle was telling me he was sorry for anything he'd ever done to me and just about everybody else in his life.

After that nobody touched me or Python again, and after a year and then another year it was never just me. It was me and Python. When I went outside he was there, next to me, my hand on his back leaning a little. When I stopped, he would stop and when I looked at something or somebody, he would look at the same thing.

In a while I didn't think about it, came to accept that he would always be there. When people talked about me, it wasn't just there goes Rocky or here comes Rocky, it was there goes Rocky and Python.

We were like one person.

Rocky and Python.

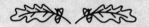

MICK

Six

BEFORE MICK there has to be something about the town because it was really the town that brought Mick. Mick called that ironic, because it was like the town caused its own destruction. Not that it was actually destroyed.

Well. Maybe it was, but not so you could see it.

I don't know much about towns. All I know is

the orphanage and Bolton, Kansas. But I watch television and read sometimes, and so I've seen other towns that way. I guess Bolton is pretty much like all of them—like Mick called it, a small version of all other places.

It has some good people and some bad people and lots in between. I probably wouldn't know anything at all except that Fred hired me to work at the elevator. Because Bolton is a farming community the elevator is the center of everything, so I got to hear about what was happening.

I think he just did it to be nice, so I'd have some spending money. He hired me to help with the books and clean up the office. During school days I worked each night after school for one hour and four hours on Saturday and Sunday we were off. But in the summer I worked each day for four hours, so I was there all the time in the dusty office next to where they brought the trucks to dump the grain through a grate to be pumped up into the elevator towers in the big auger pumps.

At first it was exciting. The farmers came in all covered with dirt and grain dust and they'd tip the trucks up to let the grain pour into the elevators. It was funny, but they would always stand in back and watch the wheat coming out, golden colored in a stream. No matter who they were, they would reach out and let the grain run through the palm of their hands.

Every time.

When I asked Fred about it he smiled and said: "It's their gold, don't you see? That's their gold and they want to touch it as it runs out."

After a while seeing the grain run, especially in the fall when the big harvest push comes on, it gets a little boring. Then I'd putz around the office and look at the stuff on the shelves. Gloves and special medicines for the cattle and blocks of salt that tasted all grainy and coarse and an old machine that took nickels to give you about a tablespoon of peanuts. It was on a hot summer day that Fred taught me about peanuts and Coke. He came in and took a bottle of Coke out of the cooler in the corner and dropped a nickel in the peanut machine and put the peanuts down in the Coke bottle.

"What's that?" I asked.

"Summer lunch—want some?"

"I never heard of such a thing."

"Maybe they didn't sell peanuts in the orphanage."

"Not Coke either."

"Try it." He handed me a Coke and dropped some peanuts in it and it wasn't bad. The salt made the Coke taste better in some way.

"See? It's just a quick bite when you feel the heat getting you down."

Except that when the farmers came in to figure up their grain Fred had a different quick bite. He kept a bottle in a sack under the counter and he would pass it to the farmer, sack and all. They would each take a shot off the bottle and snort and make faces and wheeze and spit out the door in the dust before settling down to business. The only farmer Fred didn't do the bottle in the sack with was a man named Carl Avery, who would talk about Jesus when he came. Not in a bad way, but just as he might talk about a friend—like Jesus was somebody he just met and liked—and Fred didn't hand him the bottle.

But all the rest. And when business was done

and they had figured up the amount of money due and all the government extras that would come in later, the farmers would stand and talk to Fred.

About many things.

I would sit back in the corner at the dusty desk drinking Coke with peanuts in it and listen to them talk. After a little while they forgot I was there, or maybe figured I was like the desk—almost furniture—sitting there listening to them, and I heard it all.

They loved to gossip.

They'd chew tobacco and spit in a can by the peanut machine—it's the only thing I never cleaned for Fred, that can full of spit, and it *always* seemed to be full and I *always* seemed to have to look at it—and talk about crops and who got the best wheat or the best rain or the best wife or who was fooling around with who or who owed the most money to the bank or who lost the most money in the poker game at Lyle's Weak Beer Emporium.

Fred never spoke much. He'd just smile and nod no matter what they said. I never heard him repeat a story, not once, though he had many chances.

A farmer would come in and sell wheat and tell him about some other farmer who was cheating on his income tax. Then not ten minutes after the first one was gone, the second farmer himself would come in to sell wheat, and here stood Fred, smiling and nodding, and not telling him a word about what he'd heard about how he cheated on his taxes. He'd stand there and let the man talk, never saying a word while nine times out of ten the second farmer would be telling Fred all about the first farmer and how *he* cheated on his income tax.

I used to think things were bad in the orphanage, what with one of us talking about another one, but we didn't hold anything on those farmers. I suspect it meant about as much—nothing—and I wouldn't bring it up except that it was where all the talk started that was to bring Mick.

I remember the very first time the talk started.

It was on a spring Saturday and we were selling seed. I had to write down each time a farmer bought seed because none of them had much money, and we would charge it until they could pay in the fall.

I had just entered the amount for a farmer named Packer in the charge column. Old Beebee—who worked for Fred lifting and carrying and generally anything that didn't require thinking—was taking the hundred-pound sacks of seed out to Packer's truck when Packer filled his jaw with tobacco and scratched his neck where I don't think he'd washed since maybe 1970 or '71 and said to Fred:

"Talk is we need a monument."

Like we'd heard all about it. Of course I hadn't, not in the elevator anyway, and I could tell from the way Fred was waiting that he'd never heard about it either, but he didn't say anything. Just waited for Packer to go on.

Packer spit in the can and went to the door, his hand on the knob. It didn't mean he was leaving. I've seen some of them stand with their hand on that doorknob for half an hour or more getting ready to leave, talking all the time.

He stood with his hand on the knob and said: "It's all over town that we need a monument."

Fred still didn't say anything, and I remembered now that Packer was the one other man Fred wouldn't give a drink to. I drew some squares on the blotter with the yellow wooden pencil with the name of the elevator on the side and waited, wondering what he meant by *monument*.

"It's because of that one in Washington. Word is Stanger went there on some kind of farm-subsidy trip and saw a monument and decided we had to have one, and so he come back and now everybody says we need one."

"What monument was that?" Fred asked finally. "What did he see in Washington? There's dozens of them."

"The one to the boys killed in Vietnam," Packer said. "That black wall. He saw that one and said we had to have one too."

Fred looked out the dust-covered window as a tractor went by on the way to Holsum's garage, but I don't think he was seeing the tractor. "Yes, well, Stanger had a boy that stayed in Vietnam, didn't he?"

" 'Stayed,' hell, he was killed over there."

"That's what I mean." Fred turned from the window and his eyes stopped on my face for a part of a second. They looked soft but not drunk-soft. Just soft. "That's just what I mean. Stanger lost a boy there, and I can't say I blame him for wanting a monument. It's little enough."

"Damn waste of good money," Packer said. "Good money after bad. The whole war was bad and now they want to spend more tax dollars on a monument to it. And it won't bring back Stanger's boy, nor nobody else, either, to have a black wall on the courthouse lawn."

"They're saying that?" Fred asked. "That they want a black wall?"

"Well. No. Just that we should have a monument. There's a meeting over to the courthouse Tuesday night."

"Well," Fred said, winking at me. "I guess if we're civic minded we ought to be there, oughtn't we?"

Seven

THE TRUTH was most kids wouldn't have come to the courthouse meeting about the monument, and I wouldn't have gone either except that Fred and Emma decided it was important for me to be "community minded."

Which meant I had to wear a dress. It's not that I hate dresses if there's a good reason for wearing one—say if you're going to the president's birthday party and you've got a written invitation. But usually I don't like getting into one because it leaves my leg hanging out in the open where I can see it and other people can see it.

But Emma said I had to wear one and Fred nodded and it was little enough to do for them, so Emma tied me down and got me into a yellow dress that she said set off my hair and brown eyes. To be honest about it I didn't feel bad walking between them to the courthouse. I wouldn't have admitted it to the world, but I felt all pretty and fresh and maybe strutted a little, as much as you can strut with one leg stiff, and when I turned to the side I liked the way the dress whirled out.

Python followed along behind us, walking about four feet to my rear. If I had been alone he would have walked in to my left so I could grab his shoulder hair, but for Fred or Emma he moved away and just followed.

When we got to the courthouse it was already crowded. There were pickups and cars parked in the small lot in back of the building, so many they were jammed in on top of each other and the overflow filled the street.

Python rumbled at the size of the crowd. "I didn't know there were so many people in Bolton," I said.

"Oh, my, yes," Emma answered. "If you take in all the county around there might be four, five thousand of them."

"And they're all here," Fred said, smiling. "Or almost all of them."

"They take this all pretty seriously." Emma stopped to straighten her dress, and as she bent down I could smell the wine on her breath but she didn't show it.

I put Python outside by the statues of the lions that looked more like sheep near the front door, and he sat looking out across the tops of the people coming up the steps, ignoring them.

Inside the courtroom—the largest room in town except for the gym at the school—was packed to the walls. Fred worked himself in and to the left, and we followed him until we were more or less stuck against the wall.

I couldn't see anything until Fred picked me

up and let me prop my feet on the back of one of the benches so I could see the front.

Except that there wasn't much to see. Just old Howard Bemis, the mayor, standing up at the main bench.

"The motion has been made that we hire an artist to construct a war memorial monument in front of the courthouse. This special open public meeting has been called to discuss the motion, find its merits and demerits, and open them to public scrutiny to ensure the free operation of the public will in these matters."

"For God's sake, Howard, shut up and sit down and let's get to it." This from Wayne Conners who owned a farm north of town. "I have to be home by tomorrow to work."

Howard seemed to rise on his feet. Since he was short and kind of round, it didn't do much for him except seem to raise him about half an inch. "Need I remind you, *Mr. Conners*, that this is a town matter for town residents only?"

"And need I remind you, *Mr. Bemis*, that if it weren't for my grain money and the rest of our grain money, you wouldn't *have* a town?"

"All right, all right." This came from Fred. I looked around to see him smiling. His voice was soft but everybody was listening. "That doesn't do any good at all. Let's just talk about the monument, all right?"

Which settled them right down and showed a side of Fred I didn't know about. In the elevator he just let the others talk, mostly, and didn't enter into any of it. I looked at Emma but she didn't seem surprised.

"Very well," Howard said. "Back to the issue at hand. The floor is open to discussion. Does anybody have anything to say about the war memorial?"

Which was about like throwing raw meat into the middle of a bunch of cats. *Everybody* had something to say about it, and they all said it at once. You couldn't make out any words, just a roar, and Howard held up his hands. It seemed to take about half an hour but finally everybody quietened down again.

"We'll do it by hands," he said. "You first, Margaret."

Margaret Balen stood up from one of the

benches in the front row and took a deep breath. She said all at once, "Just so it's big I think it ought to be big because there are so many small monuments in the world and we want a big one so people don't laugh at us when they drive through town." She sat down abruptly.

"Yes. Well." Howard nodded. "And you, Taft—what do you have to say?"

Taft was a man with no hair at all on his head except for bushy eyebrows and he coughed and said, "I think we ought to know how much money we're talking about here."

And so it went, talk and talk until my head was starting to nod. Fred put me down so I could sit on the back of the bench and lean against his chest and doze a little until it was over at last. I heard Howard say:

"All right, it's settled. We do the monument as long as it falls under two thousand dollars. Mrs. Langdon will see about contacting an artist since she was the one who won last year's art award at the county fair with her macramé piece depicting the history of Bolton County up to the present." He banged the gavel and we all shuffled out and worked our way into the street.

Python was waiting and slipped in behind us as we came out.

"I don't know about all this," Emma said. "Just because she could knot some baling twine into the shape of Bolton County doesn't mean Trudy Langdon can find an artist."

"Magazines," Fred said. "She's got tons of art magazines. Carl told me one day he about blew a truss moving them. She's got crates of them. There's probably ads in all of them for artists looking to do monuments."

"Still . . ."

"It will be fine, Emma, just fine."

And of course it turned out to be, but not quite in the way Fred meant it.

Eight

A WEEK PASSED, then another one, and summer rolled into the busiest part of itself. The elevator was humming, sometimes with trucks waiting in line to bring the grain in and dump it and go back for more. Farmers worked until dark, and Fred stayed open often until midnight or later so they could bring in the last trucks of grain for the day. Then the next morning they would start at daylight and we'd have to be open not long after then to be ready for them, truck after truck rolling in to dump their golden grain, the dust so thick even inside the office you could choke on it, and no way to stop.

There was so much paperwork that I had to be there almost all the time with Fred just to keep up, totaling the grain amounts and filing them in the old wooden filing cabinets next to the peanut machine.

I didn't think it would ever end, and I took to taking morning walks just after we opened the doors. There was a short quiet time just at dawn before the trucks started to come in from the fields, just an hour or so, and I would take Python and we would walk through the town. Bolton was so small that after a couple of times you'd think you knew it all but there was always something different happening. The birds were always singing and the sun wasn't hot yet and I wasn't covered with grain dust yet and Python seemed to like it. I let him pick the way to go, just moving along next to me, his shoulder against my leg, and on one of the morning walks he took me so that I met the artist Mrs. Langdon had sent for to make the war memorial.

Mick.

Although at first I didn't know he was the artist.

At first I just thought he was a pervert.

Python and I always walked a different way. Sometimes we'd move through the small downtown area because Hopper's bakery would be taking out the first rolls of the day. The smell of fresh bread came out of the back doors of the bakery into the alley and made our mouths water. Hopper would come to the door and give us each a roll, and Python would take his ever so gently, and we'd eat them hot and steaming.

Sometimes we'd go down in back of Lyle's Weak Beer Emporium because Lyle had a thing about cats and must have had a dozen of them, and Python liked to put them up the power poles. He didn't catch them and maybe even didn't want to, but it was fun for him once in a while to decorate the power poles with them, and it probably kept the cats from getting too careless.

This morning Python had taken me by the bakery and Hopper had given us each a sticky cinnamon roll. Python wasn't much on manners so he'd taken his down kind of in one gulp. I ate mine slower, and when I was done my hands were all over sticky so I let Python lick them. We were standing at one end of the alley, and I looked up while he was licking my hands, and there was Mick.

Actually there was an old station wagon with rust so bad it looked to be falling apart. The back window was rolled halfway down and the left front fender was patched over with silver duct tape until you couldn't see anything but tape. Jammed into the driver's-side window was the bottom of a man.

It had clothes on, the bottom, but there it was, filling the window, and I stopped. Python made that sound low in his throat so you thought the ground was shaking.

I knew all about perverts from what the nuns had told us—or sometimes hadn't told us—in the orphanage and also what we learned in school so I thought naturally I was seeing a pervert.

I also thought—just as naturally—how that pervert would feel if I let Python go and he took about half of that bottom off for a snack to follow up his cinnamon roll.

But something held me back. It didn't seem right for a pervert to be sitting with his bottom propped in the side of an old station wagon window at dawn in Bolton, Kansas.

Plus it wasn't moving.

"It's dead maybe," I said to Python. "It's a dead bottom."

Python rumbled again.

I moved closer.

I know how that sounds. Stupid. Everybody says if you see a pervert get away from him, and everybody is right. But I moved closer. Maybe it was because I was dumb or maybe because I half figured nobody in his right mind would bother me with Python standing next to me. Whatever the reason I moved closer.

Two steps, then two more.

Still the bottom didn't move. Just stood there

in the window. I thought maybe the joke was bad because somebody really *was* dead, the way it was so still.

When I was ten feet away it moved. Just a bit to the side, a lean, and I heard a moan, so low there was almost a chop to it, kind of, "Oh-oh-oh . . ."

Then there was a fumbling sound, a click as somehow he reached back through between his legs and operated the door handle. The door creaked open and I was looking at a man standing on his head in the front seat of the station wagon looking at me back between his knees.

Only he didn't see me. He saw Python.

"Oh God, it's death, death coming for me. I've gone too far this time. I'm gone. Gone."

Then he saw me, looking still up and back through his legs, and he smiled—that is his mouth seemed to smile, upside down—and he coughed. "Tell me—are you with death?"

I didn't say anything. It still was in my mind that he was a pervert, and I was ready to run or put Python on him, either one.

"No," he answered himself. "Death wouldn't

come with a girl. Why, then, why are you with that . . . that thing?"

"It's not a thing. It's a dog. His name is Python, and if you're a pervert, he's going to make lunch out of your rear end."

"Pervert?"

"Yes."

"Well, I've been called lots of things and will be called many more but pervert isn't one of them."

"How is it, then, that you're standing upside down in a car with your bottom sticking out the window if you're not a pervert?"

"It was the way I happened to be," he said, "when I fell asleep."

Passed out, more likely, I thought but I didn't say anything. Hell, I thought, any old pervert worth his salt wouldn't tell you if he was a pervert anyway. He'd just wait and do his pervert things, and I thought for half a second about turning Python loose anyway, just on general principle, when the man suddenly moved. His feet had been propped somehow on the ledge next to the door, and with the door open there wasn't anything to hold them on the ledge and they slipped off.

Both feet—he was wearing tennis shoes that looked to be made of rags—dropped to the ground, the legs and bottom followed, and he bounced off the seat with his face, kicked sideways off the back of the car seat, rolled half over and was sitting on the ground by the car looking up at me right side up.

"Hello." He squinted. "My eyes are bleeding."

"No they're not. You're just drunk."

"Not true. I was drunk. Now I'm not. And my eyes are bleeding. You wouldn't have a bottle somewhere, would you?"

"No." I thought of Fred's bottle at the elevator but didn't say anything about it. "You don't need it anyway."

I think I was going to say more about how he drank too much but he wasn't listening to me.

"God, look at that. See the light?"

"What light?"

"There! The light coming by that old wall, see how it comes down gold and across your face? Oh, God, see it, see the light? It comes down across you like a blessing, like a kiss from the gods. I've got to get it . . . get it. Stay there. Just there. Stay there. Don't move."

And all the time he was talking he had moved around to the rear of the car and was rummaging in the back of the station wagon, pulling at what looked like a bunch of junk to me, folders and boxes and paper sacks. In a few seconds he found a tablet and a small box that he brought to the hood of the car.

"Don't move, don't move."

I had no intention of moving. It was coming to me now, what he was, the thought, and I was wondering what it would do to Bolton.

He looked kind of like a garden gnome, one of the statues that Clyde Frenser had in his yard and garden. Round and short with red faces, all smiling, all happy, but with some little thing in their eyes, some wicked little thing that made them look like they were always on the edge of doing something wrong. His eyes had the same look, the tip up at the corners, and he had a small beard and was bald on top and looked all mussed and devilish. Even his clothes looked like they came off a garden gnome. He had a bright red shirt over a pale green pair of stretch slacks that looked like they'd been on him for about a year. There were stains down the front of his shirt that I didn't care to look at or think about much. He opened the box to show a bunch of pieces of colored chalk.

He flipped the top of the tablet back to get to a clean piece of paper and grabbed a chunk of dark-colored chalk from the box and drew.

"Don't move—not a muscle."

He sketched fast, his head bent over the tablet, his hand flying in great motions, round and round, and when I leaned forward to see he yelled at me.

"Don't *move!*"

Python rumbled at the way his voice jumped but he didn't even notice that, didn't notice death. He just kept sketching.

"The light—see the light?" His voice was a whisper while he worked, a hushed sound, almost like praying, and in a few minutes he was done.

"There—I've caught it. Just notes, see, just

notes, but I can paint it later if I can find somewhere in this place with light, with a room to work in. That's it, don't you see? Just a dry room and light. God, light is everything."

And here a strange thing happened. While he was talking, his voice soft about light and how he needed a dry room, while he was going on Python walked over to him and put his jaw against the man's leg, just pushed his muzzle over, and the gnome reached down and petted him. Without losing a finger. Python had never let another soul touch him and here he walks right up to this complete stranger who could have been a pervert and lets him touch him on the head.

"You're the artist," I said. "The one they sent for to do the monument."

"Mick," he said. "Mick . . . well, any last name you want. Just Mick. It doesn't matter. Names don't matter, do they? Only the light matters, the light and the way colors move in the light. That's all. And shapes. Line—it's all in the line."

And all this time he's petting Python, rubbing

his head. "But aren't you the one for the monument?"

"Well, that goes, doesn't it? What in bluebonnet hell would I be doing in this place if I weren't sent for? I know nothing of farming or wheat or flatness. Only line, and color and form and shading. See—look now, turn and *look,* girl, at the light coming across the face of that building. Look at how it catches the bricks so you can see the soul of the men who laid them, see the guts of the men who made the building. *See?* There it is."

And he turned to a new page in the tablet and started to draw again. This time he wasn't doing me so I could move, and I stood in back of him and watched him draw. It didn't make any sense—the lines seemed to fly all over the place, all in browns and reds and yellows, sometimes one over the other and all mixed. I didn't see how it could make anything but junk, just junk, and suddenly it did.

Suddenly it was all there. All the dust and light from the sun and the bricks in the old Emerson building that used to be a hardware store but now was empty—all of it was there. And the light.

"I can see it!" I said. "I can really see it—how did you do that?"

"It's not me, is it—it's the light. It's the way the thing is, the way of it, and I just make it be the way it is. Like over there, over by that old fence, see how it comes out there and the shadows fall in the dirt by the road?"

And he was off again, the pad out in front of him this time, his fingers holding different pieces of chalk as he moved. Python followed and I followed and watched him work. Once when I looked down, Python was looking at the chalk as well, watching it fly around the paper.

"How did you get here?" I asked. "I mean, if you see all these things to draw all the time, how do you get anywhere?"

He stopped and looked at me. "Ahh, yes, there it is, isn't it? I haven't a clue. Drunk, I suppose—drunk is the only way I can seem to get anywhere. I have a drink now and then."

"You do." I thought of Fred and Emma. They "had a drink now and then." Mick must swim in it. When he moved now I could sometimes smell him, smell his clothes, and Python didn't seem to mind. But then Python liked to roll on dead skunks on the highway when he could find them. Mick's clothes made me want to stop breathing.

But I followed him. Even the smell didn't stop me.

He kept moving and I kept following him.

Nine

SOMETIMES you don't see things and time will go by and by and then you'll look and see it. In the orphanage we always thought Sister Gene Autry was kind of ugly because she had such a square face and big jaw. But later and still later after I was adopted by Emma and Fred and woke up every morning happy, later I would sit and think of Sister Gene Autry as being kind of beautiful. And maybe she wasn't, but that's how I remember her now. I wrote a letter to her to tell her, sort of, without telling her how I thought she was beautiful now, but it embarrassed me and I never did mail it. But I wished I had. Although that's not the same.

That's what happened now, while I was following Mick. I'd been in Bolton for years, and what with walking now every morning while we worked through the hard part of harvest, I thought I knew everything about it, how it looked and acted, but I was wrong. I didn't know anything. Not really.

Mick went through town like a chalk storm, the little colored bits in one hand and the tablet in the other.

"The town, see, it's all there, all . . . right . . . there."

And he would stop and draw. Once he drew the corner, just the corner, of Henderson's old white house. It was an abandoned house on the stretch of Third and Elm. I always just thought of it as an empty house, just a box that nobody used any longer. Fred had told me once that there had been a large, happy family there but hard times had come in the thirties and they had all left, and nobody ever heard of them again, not a word.

Somehow that came into the drawing. I watched Mick work, saw the lines happen and the colors and, just from the corner of the old house, felt all the loneliness of the family being gone—all of it. It made me think of Sister Gene Autry and I swore to myself I would write her another letter and mail it this time, and Mick moved on.

On a back street he stopped by a small green house where Mr. Jennings lived. Mr. Jennings was so old that not even Fred and Emma knew how long he'd been in Bolton. Fred thought he was over a hundred and when I watched Mr. Jennings come out for mail once, to the box on the street, I agreed. It seemed to take him about a week to walk out and walk back, and he had this old, old dog named Rex who slept on the front steps. Rex would get up and walk with Mr. Jennings out to the street for the mail, step by step, and together they made you think of old—old dusty dead and *old*.

Mick did a drawing of Rex on the porch, and Rex didn't move even though Python was there which sometimes made Rex raise his head, and when he was done I could see Rex as a young dog.

He was still old and not moving and the house was still small and green and Mr. Jennings was still old but I could in some way see them all young and new. I could see Rex how he must have been when he was young with tall shoulders and pretty fur and bright eyes. The drawing made me want to know Mr. Jennings young, know what he was like when he was a young man. I decided just because of the drawing to ask around and find out all I could about him.

"How do you do that?" I asked, but he ignored me, kept going and drawing until I realized that I was late for work and Fred would have to handle the paperwork for the loads without me. He could do it, but it made things slower, and the farmers would have to wait in line longer. That made them mad because they wanted to get back to their fields.

"I have to go," I said, but he was doing a tree limb near the school, just a limb that hung out over the elementary playground fence, and he didn't hear me, or didn't care, and I turned to go.

Python didn't come.

"Are you staying with him?" I asked. It was the first time he'd ever done that, stayed when I got ready to leave. He turned at last and came to me, leaned in so I could take his shoulder. We walked four blocks back to the grain elevator while Mick stayed to draw the town.

There was a long line of trucks and Fred looked all frazzled.

"I was about to send somebody to find you."

I slid in behind the desk. "The man came— the artist."

"Oh—he did? When?"

"Must have been last night sometime. I found him asleep in his station wagon."

"In his car? Didn't he know they had a room saved for him at Carlson's bed and breakfast?"

"I guess not." Or maybe he did, I thought. Widow Carlson had heard about a new thing for small towns—bed-and-breakfast inns—on some television show she'd seen and decided she should turn her house into one.

"Just to pick up a few dollars," she said to Fred and Emma in the grocery store one day when we were shopping. "To help tide a woman over, you know, the rough spots."

Fred told me later the Widow Carlson had about as much money as a small European country, having owned seven square miles of prime wheat land that her husband left to her. Maybe she just needed something to do.

The problem was Bolton is off the path to just about anywhere in the world, and nobody ever came except grain and cattle buyers. They spent the nights in Lyle's Weak Beer Emporium until near morning, buying and selling grain and cattle, and then driving on without actually sleeping the night anywhere. So when nobody came Widow Carlson just more or less saved the breakfast portion for the next time—which was two hard-boiled eggs—and, like Fred once said, the eggs must have hair on them by this time.

Sticking Mick in there would just about kill him, especially if he tried to eat one of the eggs.

"Maybe we should go find him," Fred said. "And tell him where to go."

I shrugged. "He was over by old man Jennings's place last I saw him."

"What was he doing over there?"

"Drawing."

"Drawing pictures?"

I nodded. "Looks like he's going to draw the whole town unless he runs out of paper."

"Just drawing pictures as he goes?"

"Yup." The dust was coming into the office bad now from the dumping trucks, and I used my fingers to clean out the corner of my eyes. "His hands just fly."

"Is that a fact?" Fred stopped with his handkerchief halfway to blowing his nose. "Are the drawings good?"

I thought a minute. "I don't know. I think they are, but I don't know anything about what makes a good drawing. I know this—they make you think, make me see things I hadn't seen before. He did a drawing of old man Jennings's dog Rex, and I saw Rex like he must have been when he was young."

Fred blew his nose, then carefully folded his handkerchief and put it away. "You know, I'd like to see that—I really would."

"I could take you if you didn't have all this to do. He's just three blocks away."

He looked at me. "What do you think?"

"Fred, there's three trucks waiting."

"We'll take 'em with us."

"We will?"

"Sure. There might not be a chance to see something like this again ever."

He thought a minute, then took three cold Cokes out of the machine, poured half of each one out the window and filled them from the bottle in the sack and walked out the door.

One truck was dumping grain—there was a farmer named Hansen there—and two more were waiting. He handed Hansen one of the Cokes, went to the other two farmers and gave them each a Coke and talked to each of them a little. Pretty soon I was walking down the street with Python by my side and four big men following along behind.

We had to walk past the hardware and grocery, then along the side of Bemis's all-service station. Five people walking like that attracted attention so we picked up one here and one there until I looked back and we had nine men and three women following, none of them talking, just following in the early morning behind Python and me.

We found Mick another block down from where he'd been. He was doing a drawing of an old car up on blocks in back of Harrison's house. It was an old Ford, and Mick was leaning the tablet against a tree while he worked. I stopped in back of him and watched him draw. All the people with me formed a rough circle around in back of me and if Mick saw us or even knew we were there, he made no sign. His fingers whipped the chalk around, and the car came into being on the paper. When he came to doing the small oval emblem that said Ford in written letters I heard somebody in back of me cough and say:

"You know, when Harrison was young, he went to sparking in that car and he used to shine it and shine it so the emblem just stood out, caught the light and stood out. Just like on that drawing. How could that be?"

And so it did. And when he was done with the old car he moved on. Only this time he didn't fold the drawing into the tablet but tore it from the pad. He handed it to Fred who took it, looked at it, and passed it on to the rest of the people.

There was no sound except their breathing. I thought it might be because they didn't like the drawing but it was the other way. They saw what I saw, or thought I saw—saw that the drawings were more than just drawings. Were somehow *inside* of what they were drawings of, so that they showed all of what that thing had been or would be.

Showed not just the old car, but in some strange way what made the thing that way, how it lived and maybe died.

Mick was drawing now by Harrison's mailbox, how it leaned out and over the curb, the way the shadow from it went. His hands started the big, looping movements to form things in when he suddenly stopped.

His nose went in the air.

"Could it be," he said, "that there is something drinkable nearby?"

Fred nodded and held out the Coke bottle he was carrying.

"No, no, I didn't mean anything sweet."

Fred said nothing, just held the Coke bottle out. Something in his eyes went to Mick and Mick nodded and took the bottle and drank back about half of it.

"There." He sighed. "I've been a touch off since I woke up this morning in that strange position and that helps. That helps."

He studied us as if seeing us for the first time. "Now, tell me, where did you all come from?"

Ten

IT CAME TO ME that night that I should be
an artist.

Well—not that fast. It wasn't just one of those
silly things you hear about where somebody
watches a video and decides to be a rock star or
a rodeo rider or an airline pilot. Not wacky like
that, or not like we used to do in the orphanage
when we would study pictures in magazines

and try to imagine how it would be to live the way they lived in the pictures.

It was not from what Mick was doing, not from how he lived—not that. Who wants to live in a rusty old station wagon drunk all the time with your rear end sticking out the window and not knowing where you are?

It was something else. Not something that Mick did so much as what his work made me want to do.

If I could have wrapped the rest of that first day in plastic and kept it in a box forever to take out and look at and play with, I would have been happy.

Mick moved through the whole town. The grown-ups left after a little time to get back to what they were doing, and I started to follow them as well—Python stayed with Mick again and I had to call him to break him away—but Fred stopped me.

"The elevator will run fine without you for a while if you want to stay."

"It's all right. He's just going to draw more pictures and what is that to watch?"

But he knew, Fred knew that I really wanted to see it, see all of it, and he shook his head. "Things like this come along, you've got to see them. 'Specially if you're young. You stay and I'll keep up as best I can. Then you can tell me all about it at supper tonight. You be my eyes."

So I stayed with Mick almost the rest of the day until Mrs. Langdon found him.

Until then he just kept moving, working, drawing so that he filled the tablet, and when it was full he turned it over and started to draw on the backs of the papers he'd already drawn on. It didn't matter to him.

Once he saw something small, some little thing I couldn't see. He lowered to his hands and knees and crawled into a shrub by the Walters's place dragging the tablet behind him.

"What are you doing?"

"Come see—come see. Oh, it's the most lovely thing, the most lovely, lonely thing of all. Come see."

I didn't want to crawl into any old bush. The Walterses had about seven dozen kids from diaper-fillers to older than me, and the older ones had a way of teasing that made me not want to embarrass myself.

But Python followed him in. I couldn't let Python follow where I wouldn't go so I scrabbled down—it was hard because of my leg—and I looked in. Light came down through the bush and showed on a small place, just a little circle inside the bush, and there was a tiny cross made of popsicle sticks where one of the Walters kids had buried a gerbil or a dead bird.

It didn't matter what was buried there. Not to Mick. He pulled the pad in with him, and I watched him make the light and the little circle and the two crossed popsicle sticks. While he worked I saw his face and he was crying.

Tears moving down through the grime of sleeping in the car and the dust under the bush, crying while he worked until he was done. I could see it then, see the sadness of the little grave and the way the light hit the popsicle sticks. When we were walking down the sidewalk with the cracks where the elm tree roots were pushing up, I asked him about it.

"How could you see that? Where the Popsicle-stick grave was? It didn't show, I couldn't see it until I got in there—how could you see that walking by on the sidewalk?"

He stopped and scratched his hair around the bald spot with his fingernails. Bits of dust and dirt came out. "It had to be there, didn't it?"

"What do you mean?"

"Just that—it had to be there, didn't it? A child simply had to go in there and bury a wee bird or animal. It was the place it had to be and I knew it was there. Just as I know this woman coming is after me—not you."

I turned and there came Mrs. Langdon, walking so fast the band that went around her head to hold her glasses almost flew out in back of her hair.

"Mr. Strum," she yelled, half a block away. "Oh, Mr. Strum, I didn't know you'd arrived."

"Who is she?" He scratched his stomach, which was covered with different-colored stripes of chalk where the board had left marks while he worked.

"Mrs. Langdon," I said.

"Ahh, the one who wrote me." He nodded.

"It's not good," he said aside to me, his voice lowered, "when they call you *Mr.* that way. Only people who want something call you that—bill collectors. Or rich bankers who want you to make their nose look better than it is. It was either Oscar Wilde or Whistler or Sargent who said an oil portrait is a painting with something wrong with the mouth. Or was it the nose? Silly, isn't it?" But he turned toward her and smiled.

"Hello."

"Mr. Strum," Mrs. Langdon said—it was the first time I'd heard his last name. "Mr. Strum, when did you arrive?"

Mick looked at me, a question in his eyes.

"Last night," I said. "I think he got here last night. He was here this morning. Sleeping in his car." I did not add how he was sleeping.

"But you were supposed to contact me when you arrived. We had a nice room for you at Carlson's bed and breakfast."

"It was necessary," Mick said, rising on his feet, "to capture the ambience of the town, the soul of the town. I could hardly have done that in the comfort of a soft bed."

"Of course, of course."

But I could tell that he wasn't serious. His voice had changed and out of the corner of his eye I thought I saw him wink at me. Still, he smiled at Mrs. Langdon and nodded.

"I will accompany you now," he said, "as soon as I pay my assistant."

He looked back through the tablet and tore loose the drawing of Jennings's dog Rex and handed it to me. "For you."

"But I didn't do anything."

"More than you know, more than you'll ever know."

In the orphanage when you got something you didn't argue about it. There weren't that many things to come your way but I was trying to change some of those things from the way I did them back then. Like grabbing at food or thinking of myself all the time. But I held back the once and that was enough.

"Thank you."

"You're very welcome. I will need your assistance again on the morrow. Perhaps you could meet me, along with your trusted companion"—

he pointed to Python—"in the morning at the aforementioned bed and breakfast—say at eight o'clock?"

I had to work of course. I couldn't leave Fred alone at the grain elevator. But I thought that if I went for the rest of the afternoon and evening and straightened the books out maybe I could take some time in the morning—"on the morrow"—to meet Mick and help him.

"I'll try."

"Very good." He turned to Mrs. Langdon. "And now, my dear, proceed."

I watched them until they were near the corner. Mrs. Langdon was tall, and he was short—came just over her shoulder, and she bent to talk to him, her finger wagging and her head shaking—and it looked like somebody walking with a messy pet. Chalk dust seemed to poof off him with each step, and he was stained from the work, the drinking, the sleeping in the car. Just before he was out of hearing I remembered something.

"Don't eat the eggs," I called. "They're older than you."

But he didn't hear me.

The rest of that day I worked at the elevator and brought all the books up to the minute and had them all ready so Fred could just enter things the next morning. We went home late and I took a hot bath and sat in my bed in my pajamas and looked at the drawing Mick had given me and decided to be an artist.

It was there—in the drawing. But in more, too, in the way it had been today watching him work, watching him see things, see inside them. I put the drawing on a piece of cardboard and leaned it against the mirror on my little birch dressing table. I watched it until I was nearly asleep, remembering how he had done the lines, the colors, how he worked the chalk with his fingers to make Rex be something on the paper.

Before I slept there was a soft knock on the door, and Fred and Emma were there to say good night as they did each night before I went to sleep. It reminded me somehow of the orphanage because Sister Gene Autry always came in to say good night to us the same way.

Emma tucked me in and Fred ruffled my hair and I lay back on the pillow.

"I'm going to be an artist," I said.

"It couldn't go any other way," Fred said, nodding. "Ain't he something?"

"It's not just him," I said. "It's the drawing, all of it."

"I know," Emma said. "You just let it grow and grow and have a good time with it. That's the most important thing." She leaned down and kissed me on the forehead and touched my cheek with her hand that smelled of lilac water. Fred turned off the light so I could sleep but I lay awake for a long time and stared at the drawing in the light that came in the window from the streetlight. It changed and changed until I thought it was moving, and then I went to sleep.

Eleven

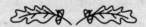

HE WAS NOT the same person in the morning.

I woke up with the sun and had breakfast with Fred and Emma and went with Fred to the elevator to help start up.

At seven twenty Python and I left the elevator and walked to Carlson's place where his station wagon was parked. At exactly eight o'clock he came out the door with a pad of paper and a small wooden box that I found was a pencil case. He was scrubbed clean, had on fresh baggy canvas pants and a clean white shirt with the sleeves rolled up to the middle of his upper arms. The hair around his bald spot was slicked back with water. His eyes looked clear.

"Good morning," he said, then down to Python, "and to you too. How are you both this morning?"

"We're fine. I want to be an artist." It just popped out and I wished I hadn't said it because it sounded silly, but he said a strange thing.

"And how could it be any other way?" It was almost exactly the same thing Fred had said the night before.

"Can you . . . teach me?"

He shook his head. "No. Not to be an artist. You already are that—I knew you had the hot worm in you when I first saw you walking up to the station wagon."

"I didn't think you could see much with your—from that end."

"Well, then, there's seeing," he smiled, "and

there's *seeing,* isn't there? The point is I knew it, and there is nothing I—nor you, for that matter—can do about it. The fact exists. You are an artist."

"But I don't know anything."

"Ahh, there I can help you." He paused and let gas, just as natural as anything, and rubbed his stomach. I don't think he thought it was crude or even thought of it at all—maybe nothing was crude to him. "She had strange eggs for breakfast—reminds me of some I had in India once. They were pickled but these had the strangest flavor."

I didn't say anything. If they hadn't killed him by now they probably wouldn't.

"I can teach you something of technique, of line, of color—of art." He stopped at the station wagon and opened the back, put the pad and pencils in the back in a pile of what looked exactly like junk. He closed the rear door and motioned to the door on the passenger side.

"Get in. Your lesson starts now."

"Where are we going?"

"Tomorrow night there is to be a public meeting to make some kind of decision about the monument. I need to know more about your town, my dear, more of what it's like so that I can decide what kind of a monument to do."

"But isn't that up to them? To the people in the town?" I held the door open and Python climbed into the front seat and sat in the middle. I climbed in and sat in the middle of a junk pile of old cans, bread wrappers, and empty potato chip bags, and some stuff I didn't want to guess about. Python seemed to love it. "Don't the people in Bolton get to decide what kind of monument they get?"

He looked at me, watched my face. "You're serious, aren't you?"

I nodded. "It seems like if they're paying for it . . ."

"There it is—right there." He slammed his hand against the wheel and I felt Python jump next to me. "There's the crux of it, isn't it? All of art comes down to that, right down to that." He laughed but it wasn't a funny laugh, more a sad one. "You have to kind of squirm around that point—like a bug on a hot stove looking for a cool place. That's art, that is. Right there."

He was silent for a time, which was just as well. The station wagon, once it got moving, sounded like it was going to explode. Things clunked and rattled and the muffler must have been gone because it was impossible to hear anything but a loud yell.

Which Mick did now. He leaned across Python, close to my ear, and yelled:

"Art is like medicine—people take it because they have to take it, because they *think* they have to take it or because you *make* them think they have to take it. True art, that is." He took a deep breath, yelled again, "If we left it up to them we'd be waist deep in bleeding pictures of Elvis or Christ on black velvet in no time."

He had been driving all the while, and we went past the north edge of town on County Road 1. When we were about a mile out of town Mick turned the wagon into a driveway and backed out so he was facing Bolton and cut the engine.

It looked peaceful in the morning light. The

elevators stood like statues, tall and white, on the right edge of town. The water tower stood on the left side and the trees hid most of the rest of it. You could see white here and there where a house showed through and one line of red where Carlson's brick house stood.

"You can't see people," I said. It was nice with the station wagon engine stopped—I felt like my ears were bleeding. "Not a soul."

"For a start—to know the place. Without people. It's about people who are gone, isn't it?"

"What do you mean?"

"The monument—the whole idea of it. It's about dead people, not living ones, isn't it? So we have to see how it looks without people."

He sat for a time, just looking at the town, and I tried to do it the same way, and even Python seemed to be trying. His big muzzle aimed out over the hood and he watched the town but he soon became bored, and so did I.

"What are we looking for?" I asked.

"Nothing."

"That's what I've been seeing."

"Keep looking. This is your first lesson."

He reached around in back of the seat and found the tablet and pencils he'd thrown in earlier. He handed them to me.

"What's this?"

"Draw."

"But I don't know anything about drawing."

"Draw."

"What should I draw?"

"Draw."

"You brought this for me, didn't you?"

He nodded.

"But that was before I told you I wanted to be an artist."

Another nod.

"How did you know?"

"It doesn't matter. Open the pencils. Draw."

I looked down at the pencil box. It felt very old. Made of polished wood, so worn the grain seemed to be raised. It had a sliding top and I slid it back to see eight or ten wooden pencils, all different sizes and lengths. "How old is it— the box?"

"When I was a boy I had it and it was old then—it doesn't matter." He pointed to the pencils. "Some are soft and some are hard. Some can be used for shading. Draw."

"The town?"

"What you see. Draw."

So I drew the elevators. They were the biggest thing to see, and they stood up with all sorts of straight lines that were easy to make except that when I was done, it just looked like a bunch of straight lines.

"See now, see how she does the lines," he said, looking up at the sky. "She does the lines so well."

"But it doesn't look right. It doesn't look like the elevators."

"See?" He took the drawing and used a wide pencil to shade one of the elevator sides to make it look deep and it just about jumped off the paper.

"There."

"I see."

"Draw."

I did some shading and it worked. The elevator grew out from the page, looked closer to what it was—round and full of grain.

When I was done he took the tablet, looked at it for a moment, flipped the page over to show a fresh sheet and said: "Draw."

I drew four more drawings. The water tower, an overall view trying to show the trees which just looked like a bunch of blops until he showed me how to use shading and small lines to make the leaves so they looked like trees, then one of the edge of the Carlson house, and one of the highway going into town.

He nodded his head when I finished each one. "You must do this and do this—for years. Draw and draw until you think your hands will fall off. Just to know the line—the way the line works."

"What about color—all the rest of it?"

"It's because you're young, isn't it—the impatiences? The small impatiences." He nodded. "That's fine—just fine. It's all right to be impatient as long as you keep working. But remember that—to keep working. Work is all there is, all of everything. That's enough from here."

I put the pencils back into the box and he put the pad and pencils in the back of the wagon again. The engine roared again.

"Where are we going now?" I yelled.

"Graveyard."

"Oh good," I said, but he didn't hear me.

He seemed to know things—knew just how to drive to the graveyard, which was on the south edge of town, opposite from the way we had been.

I don't know about other small towns but Bolton takes care of its graveyard. I had never been there except to walk past, but the grass is always mowed and it's always clean and neat. Many of the graves have plastic flowers by them.

Mick stopped the wagon by the entrance to the graveyard. "Get your pad and pencils."

He walked down the small road that led into the graves and I followed, Python at my side.

About in the middle of the graveyard Mick stopped, looking around. "The old section— where's the old section?"

I didn't know, but after a moment of standing rubbing his nose, he nodded and walked down a side path to some older-looking headstones.

"Here. The old ones are the best."

"Best at what?"

"Best to tell us what the town is really like—how the soul is. There, look at the stones, how they're different from the others."

And they were. The newer stones were just square blocks with the names carved out, sometimes stacked on another square block. Here, in the old part, there were sculpted figures and flowers and on one little stone a lamb, lying on its side.

"See?"

I couldn't get my eyes off the small stone.

CLAIR MILLER
BORN MAY 5, 1887
TAKEN OCT. 9, 1890
SHE BIDES IN HEAVEN,
AT PLAY WITH ANGELS DEAR

"She was just a baby," I said. "Three years old."

Mick nodded. "Draw."

"Here?"

"What you see—draw."

So I drew the headstone and it was going fine until I started on the little curled-up lamb on top. It was so small and alone. I remembered the orphanage and how it had been sometimes alone in the room when I didn't think I would ever get adopted, alone like the little lamb. I wondered how Clair Miller had come to die and I started to cry.

"Ahh, yes, there it is, isn't it?"

"It's not what you think."

"Well, of course it is. You're crying, and that's the way it should be."

"I'm not crying. I don't cry." Not at the orphanage and not since the orphanage. I didn't cry. Not ever. And here I was, crying.

"It's all right to cry," he said. "I cry each day— my soul weeps. It means you're seeing something as it is, as it's meant to be seen, doesn't it? Oh, yes, crying is the thing to do." He smiled. "As long as you keep on drawing. Know the line, always that, know the line."

And I kept drawing and only dripped a little on the paper. When I finished I looked and saw that Mick was standing in front of a plain white stone, a rectangle, small and straight with no decoration.

I went to it and read:

CLELL MILLER
BORN SEPT. 8, 1843
DIED NOV. 27, 1862
INFANTRY

"Was he a soldier?"

Mick nodded. "Civil War."

"Killed in battle?"

"Maybe. Probably not. Most of them died of disease—four to one. Four soldiers in the Civil War died of dysentery—the black squirts, they called it—for every one that died of battle wounds. So he probably died that way." He sighed. "Heroes all, weren't they? All of them heroes. There were four, you know."

"Four what?"

"Four men from the Bolton area to die in the Civil War. One more in the Spanish-American War. Seven in the First World War. Three in the Second World War. One in Korea and two in Vietnam. Eighteen all told to die in war, of one thing or another—eighteen young men gone."

"How could you know that?"

He smiled. "I could say I just know it—the way I knew the popsicle-stick cross would be under the bush—but the truth is I looked it up. Military records. When the fair Mrs. Langdon wrote to me I contacted a clerk in the army and asked him to check the records. It's all in St. Louis, you know—all the army records. Eighteen dead. And they want a monument." He looked from the graveyard to the town. "I'll wager there aren't two people in town who know how many have been killed—or that there's a hero here."

"A hero?"

"Congressional Medal of Honor winner. A true hero."

"Who?"

"Mr. Jennings. I drew his dog, didn't I? I saw the name on his mailbox—that must have been him. He was a hero in the First World War. God, he must be close to a hundred."

"I didn't know."

"I don't think anybody does." He shook his head. "And we won't tell if he doesn't want it known, will we?"

"What did he do?"

"Killed some people. Killed a lot of them while

they were trying to kill him, probably—that's how they usually win those things. Although some have won it for saving people's lives—medics in combat. I don't know. Just that he won a medal and we'll let it be. Now you have to help me."

"How?"

"I need a place where the men come to sit and talk—a gathering place for them."

"That's easy," I said. "The grain elevator or the bar. Which do you want?"

"Both—but in the interests of sanity and caution perhaps we might try the elevator first. Drinking establishments have a way of . . . affecting me."

Twelve

FRED WAS SURPRISED to see me come to the elevator. We had talked it out the morning before I met with Mick.

"Seems like it's in the interests of your new career to spend some time studying with this artist," he said after breakfast.

"I'm caught up on the paperwork. I lined out all the books and stuff so you can just fill it in. I can come in the evening and finish it out for the day."

"Let's not worry too much about that—art seems to be a little more important."

"It does?" All this time and he'd never said two words about art and after breakfast he drops that.

"Yup." He smiled. "Ain't that right, Emm?"

And Emma nodded and I don't know why I was ever worried about it.

So when I showed up at the elevator with Mick, Fred raised his eyebrows. He was covered with grain dust and it made him look like a monkey.

"He wanted to come here." I shrugged. "I don't know why."

"Because this," Mick said, his arms sweeping around at the dust and the hum of machinery and the truck dumping a golden stream of wheat through the grate with Harry Clark standing by the rear end, his hand in the falling wheat and hundreds of sparrows and pigeons all over the ground getting grain. "This is the cosmic center of the universe."

"It is?"

"Draw."

He had made me carry the tablet and pencil box from the station wagon. I felt really silly taking it out to draw in front of Fred and Harry Clark. There were three more trucks that pulled up while we stood there, waiting to dump grain, and all the men and two boys who were helping their fathers came into the elevator. One of the boys was Jimmy Durbin, who I liked to look at, the way you do, and I felt shy about drawing in front of them.

But Mick looked at me. His eyes seemed to go into my brain, stopped me.

"Draw," he said again, his voice low and even. "It's what you do—draw."

I knew he was right. I had decided to be an artist sitting alone in my bed, where it was easy to say that, but the decision held out here as well—out where it showed, where people could see me.

Even if it was embarrassing.

So I went back into the corner of the office to

my desk and put the tablet down and started to draw.

I tried to draw people, the men standing there, but I couldn't get them to look right so I worked at the scene, the room, the door and the window looking out to where the truck was dumping grain. It was funny but I started to see things for the first time that I had been looking at forever.

The wood over the door. It wasn't just wood, it was beautiful with dark strips of grain that seemed to jump out even through the layers of dust from the wheat, oiled dark wood. I wondered where it came from and how it got where it was, why somebody would take so much time and effort on a piece of wood over a door. I tried to draw the wood, the door, tried to get that feeling in it. It didn't work and I looked up and Jimmy Durbin was standing there looking at the drawing.

"It's really good," he said.

I looked to see if he was teasing me—thought about turning Python loose on him if he was, maybe taking a leg—but he meant it.

"It's hard for me to do."

"That's because you're making it look good. Anybody can do it if it's easy. The hard stuff takes longer."

"I'm going to be an artist." Oh great, I thought. Stupid. Open my mouth and be stupid.

"It shows."

He smiled and moved back to his father but he looked at me two or three more times. I was glad I was sitting down so my leg was under the desk. I tried to push my hair back when he wasn't looking so it would be neater and I thought, hey, you never know, you never know. I was glad I hadn't let Python have his leg.

"You can't just do a monument, can you?" I heard Mick say. There were four men now, and one young boy named Carl who was seven or eight and hiding in back of his father's leg looking at Python with big eyes while he chewed his lower lip. I wished I could draw people because it would make a good drawing, the way he was standing.

"Monuments have to be a certain way for a certain place."

"Hell." Clyde Jamison went to the door, opened it, and spit a gob of tobacco juice that would have killed a sparrow if it had hit one. He closed the door and turned back to Mick. "Monuments is monuments. You raise something up there and a month later pigeons are crapping on it and nobody remembers anything. It's all a waste of money."

"Not this time," Mick said, his voice quiet. "Not on this one."

"What makes this one different?"

"You," he said. Then swung his arm around to the rest of the room. "All of you. Everybody in this town. They're all different from all other towns. When I know you, all of you, I'll know how to make the monument, won't I?"

A couple of them nodded. Fred did nothing, just watched, and I was glad he was my father. He just held back and studied things and always knew—always knew. How is it, I wondered for about the millionth time, that I didn't get adopted and didn't get adopted and then one day Fred and Emma came in and I got lucky, luckier than I could ever have hoped.

"So I'm trying to learn as much as I can before the day after tomorrow."

"What's day after tomorrow?"

"The meeting," Fred said. "There's a meeting at the courthouse to decide on the monument."

"Ahh, yes."

"Everybody is coming. It's a potluck."

"I'll be there—but I still think it's just some-place for pigeons to dump."

The men moved back to their trucks and Mick motioned for me to stay and work. He went back out to his wagon and found a new tablet and his bag of chalks and started to work on his own.

He began in the office with me, his hands floating over the paper in swirls before lowering. I watched him for a bit, then watched Fred watching Mick.

Fred's eyes glowed.

"It's like dancing, ain't it?" he said to me when he saw me watching him. "His hands just dance."

Some of the men came back in and watched him as their trucks dumped, watched him draw the trucks and the grain coming down and the office and the old wood and the peanut machine. I thought I would never be able to do it.

He must have known what I was thinking. "You just keep working," he said. "It will come, it will come."

"I'd rather watch you—to learn."

"That too, but work as well. Watch and learn and work and live and be."

He was looking out the window while he talked and his voice trailed off.

"The sparrows. Look at them."

He went to the window and leaned the tablet against the bottom edge so that it lay flat, and I stood to his side and saw the sparrows. They were all around the elevator—hundreds and hundreds of them, sometimes so thick they are like water when you walk, parting ahead of you and then landing again in back to get at the grain that's spilled or blown off the trucks.

I had never thought of them as pretty but Mick drew them with the chalk, just spots in the whirl of dust around the elevator so that they seemed to be moving, dancing, swirls of birds that went up from the elevator floor along the towers of concrete where the grain was stored, seemed to be alive.

"I can't see like that," I said. "Not to see them that way."

"You will—it will come. You will see that way."

It was so strange because there were other people in the room, Fred and one other man and Jimmy Durbin had just left and here we were talking like nobody else existed, and in a way they didn't.

There was just the drawing that he was doing and I was watching, and none of the other people seemed to be there, just us. All of that day we did the same—went around town seeing things, doing drawings.

Down alleys, into the bakery—where we sat in back on the loading steps and shared a package of rolls with Python—into the courthouse, the jail (which I had never seen) where the cells were empty, drawing after drawing, all his in chalk and mine in pencil until it was evening and we were standing by the station wagon.

"Tomorrow you're on your own," he said. "Do the same thing."

"What are you going to do?"

"Work. I have to prepare the presentation and that will take most of the day. And tonight there is one place I have to investigate where you can't come."

"Lyle's Weak Beer Emporium," I guessed.

"Exactly. If the grain elevator is the soul of Bolton then the pub is . . . well, some other part of the anatomy. But it needs to be studied, doesn't it?"

"I guess." I didn't actually think so. All I'd seen of the bar was when fights between big, drunk farmers after harvest was finished would boil out into the street and the sheriff would have to stop them.

"Well of course it does, of course it does. I have one other thing for you—a present—before we part."

"What is it?"

"A book . . ." He was rummaging around in the back of the wagon and he brought out a large book in a plastic garbage bag. "Here."

"What is it about?"

"It's an art book about a painter."

I looked in the bag. It was a large book a foot by a foot and a half with a colored jacket and it was in good shape, kept clean by the plastic bag. I pulled it out.

DEGAS

Just the one word, on the cover, and below the word a painting of a racehorse.

"It's beautiful—I don't know what to say. Thank you."

"Study it. I have. Work, draw, and study. We'll talk about it day after tomorrow, after the explosion."

"What explosion?"

"The one tomorrow evening at the courthouse. You're coming, aren't you?"

"I wouldn't miss it for the world."

Thirteen

THAT NIGHT I read the book, or started to read it.

Degas was a French painter who was part of something called the Impressionist Movement, which I had not studied, even in school, where the arts teacher only comes once a week on a circuit from other schools.

After working for a little time at the elevator to

help Fred—even though he said I didn't have to, I felt kind of guilty about it—I went home and ate. I took a bath in a hurry and went to my room and snuggled into the covers with a glass of Pepsi and four chocolate chip cookies that Emma had made and opened the book.

It was hard to read and the first part was all reading. I thought it would be wrong to skip it, but the letters were very small and there were lots of dates and French names so that I had trouble keeping focused on them, and I decided to move to the back of the book for a while where there were colored plates of his paintings.

"Oh."

I actually made a sound. I couldn't help it. The pictures were so good, so pretty.

There was a painting of racehorses and the colors seemed to jump off the page; you could see the muscles moving under their skin, hear the pounding, smell the sweat.

Another of a woman standing by a door, just that, but the colors and the light made it seem as if she had just walked in and was going to say something to me.

109

But even with that, even with the beauty, I was still trying to work, trying to see the colors and the way Degas had drawn things until I turned the page and just stopped, stopped dead.

It was a painting of a group of young women practicing ballet, called *The Dance Master*. The wall in the room was green and there was a big mirror on one side for the dancers to see themselves. In the background there is a raised platform or bleachers for people to sit and watch and dancers are everywhere, practicing, stretching, fixing their costumes. On one side there is an older man leaning on a cane—an instructor—and he is watching them, studying them, and still I would have been all right except for one girl.

She was standing to the side of the dancers but almost in the middle of the painting and she is watching them, worried about something, with her hand to her mouth, and I looked at her and started to cry.

She looked like me, or sort of like me, but that wasn't it—at first I didn't know why I was crying. Then I thought of what they were, all of them, dancers, and that all of what they were was gone.

The painting was done in the late eighteen-hundreds. They were all gone. All dead. I wanted to know the girl, wanted to watch them practice. I wanted to see the dresses move and hear the music, wanted to know which ones the dance master picked for performance and if the girl who looked a little like me was one of them. I wanted to talk to them and ask them how it was to wear the costumes and dance and dance and dance without one stiff leg. I wanted to know their dreams and hopes and all of them, all the girls in the drawing and the dance master and the people sitting in the bleachers and the light and maybe even the building were dead and gone. I would never know their names or their favorite colors or what kind of music they liked or what they thought of school or what they had for supper. Gone, gone, gone.

So I cried, thinking of it, and must have made a sound because the door opened and Emma came in and sat on the bed.

"What's wrong?" she asked.

"The picture," I said. "They're all gone and I want them to not be gone." And I explained what I meant while Emma sat there and nodded and pushed the hair back from my face and smiled and wiped my cheeks where the tears went down.

"Just gone," I said, finishing. "They're all gone."

Emma shook her head. "But they aren't, don't you see? There's still the painting, isn't there? You have that. You will always have the picture, won't you? So they can never be gone."

And of course she was right.

The painting.

There was still and would always be the painting. Emma turned out the light and I lay back on the pillow with the book on the stand next to the bed and went to sleep thinking I would find Mick in the morning and tell him what I had learned from the book on Degas.

The painting. There would always be the painting.

Fourteen

PYTHON WAS WAITING for me when I came out in the morning, but not sitting the way he usually did. He was standing by the door, waiting, and as soon as we reached the sidewalk he started leading me.

"What are you doing?" He was taking me toward the center of town and I wanted to go to

Carlson's bed and breakfast, the opposite direction, so I let him go.

He stopped.

"You're going the wrong way."

He waited, watching me, his tail flopping.

"We're going this way."

But he didn't turn. He had never done this before, fought me this way, so I decided there must be a reason. I went to him and grabbed the fur on his shoulder and followed the way he wanted to go.

Toward downtown, but off to the side, into an alley and then another alley, and we came to the back of Lyle's Weak Beer Emporium.

He was there looking sort of the same as the first morning when I saw him.

His behind was sticking up in the air, his front end was jammed down in some boxes and garbage so that I couldn't see his face, and there was no movement.

Mick.

He looked like he'd been thrown in the trash and for a minute I thought he was dead. I let go of Python and walked up to where he was crumpled.

"Mick?"

There was a sound—like air coming out of a tire—and I saw the rear end move.

"Are you all right?"

"No." The voice was muffled, coming from inside the garbage. "Do I look all right?" He rolled sideways—fell over—and brushed napkins and coffee grounds and beer cans and worse out of his face. "Tell me, do you have a gun?"

"Gun?" I shook my head. "No, why?"

"I was hoping somebody could come along and shoot me and end this."

His face was all puffed and smashed and bloody, both eyes swollen almost shut, the lips cracked.

"What happened?" I asked, but I knew the answer.

"I'm not quite certain. It may have been something I said or something they said. One thing has a way of leading to another, doesn't it? We were all beyond reason and there was a fight and I wound up here."

"They always fight in Lyle's Weak Beer Emporium," I said. "You shouldn't have gone there."

"Nonsense—it's a very nice pub. Much nicer than many I've been in. I remember one in Sydney—my God, they had ball bats in Sydney. They very nearly killed me for talking about one of their dogs—I think they were collies." He rose to his feet, staggering and wobbling, his clothes half torn off.

"You look awful."

"In the name of art," he said. "All in the name of art." He looked up at the sun where it was starting to show above the roof edge of Lyle's and spit out what looked like a tooth. "What time is it?"

"I don't have a watch—I think just after seven thirty. Close to eight."

"Ahh—eleven hours until the presentation tonight. Good, right on schedule. Everything moving right along as the plan dictates."

"Plan? You mean all this"—I pointed to the garbage and the way he looked—"is part of a plan?"

"Well—I meant to win the fight, or at least do better."

"You knew there would be a fight?"

He smiled, and I was right, there was a gap where a tooth had been. "It was as sure as that little grave in the bushes, my dear. There had to be a fight, didn't there? Because there was a Lyle's and there was a me and there was that herd of animals who drink in there—of course there would be a fight."

"And you did it anyway?"

He looked at me—or tried to look at me. It was really more of a squint through the puffy eyes. "All of it, all of everything here was to be in the monument—what I like or don't like, what happens to me or doesn't happen to me doesn't matter. The art is all of it, isn't it? Don't you know that already?"

I didn't say anything but I knew he was right. I thought of the painting the night before, sitting there crying because the painting made me cry, and I knew he was right. I nodded.

"Well, then—it's all going according to plan.

Now you go on with your sketchbook and pencils and work—draw. And I'll get to business."

"What are you going to do?"

"The same as you, my dear. I'm going to draw. I'll see you at the courthouse tonight."

THE
MONUMENT

Fifteen

SEVEN O'CLOCK even in late summer in Bolton is still day, nowhere near night—it doesn't get dark for two more hours—and most people in the summer work until it's really dark. Except for the downtown people. They close up about five.

Fred usually works into the night but early that day the trucks stopped coming. I was helping Fred—I'd gone around and just about drawn everything there was to draw in Bolton and needed to talk to Mick some more to know what to do next, or how to draw better. So I'd gone to help Fred because I couldn't talk to Mick, and about five o'clock the trucks stopped. I looked out and there were no more. Fred came out of the machinery room that drove the augers to take grain into the storage bins.

He was covered with dust—half an inch thick—and he sneezed and shook it off.

"There are no more trucks," I said.

He nodded. "They're stopping for the day."

"They are?" I'd never heard of them stopping early for anything. Not unless it rained. Then they had to wait for the grain to dry out. "Why?"

"To get cleaned up for the meeting."

"Are they all coming?"

He nodded again. "Everybody I talked to will be there. Come on, let's get home and clean up and eat."

We walked home—four blocks—and you could feel something. Almost a hum. People waved and said hello and asked if we were going to the courthouse and Fred would say:

"Wouldn't miss it."

And the next person would wave and ask if we were going. Nobody knew quite what to expect, but everybody, everybody was going.

We showered and I put on clean jeans and a T-shirt with the name of a hard-rock place on it even though Emma wanted me to wear a dress. We left about six forty-five to walk down to the courthouse. Fred had a car, an old Chrysler that he baby-talked to when he drove, but he didn't use it unless we went for a special drive or had to go somewhere out of Bolton to go shopping.

It took us about five minutes to walk downtown and it's just as well we didn't try to drive. There were cars parked and jammed the whole way and crowds of people walking, all clean and neat and dressed in their Sunday clothes.

"I didn't know there were this many people who cared about art in Bolton County," I said.

"It isn't just art," Emma said. "This monument thing is more than just art. Not everybody will come, but I'd bet there will be close to a thousand."

A thousand was a lot for the courthouse.

They were packed on the steps going in so I had trouble making room for Python by the concrete lions. I kind of had to let Python look at a couple of smart-aleck boys the way he looks at chickens before they made a place for him.

The hallways were jammed and the courtroom—the biggest room in the building—was full. Men and women were trying to get in the doorway. I heard sound, voices, some saying things—it sounded angry—some just rumbling.

Fred and Emma were stopped but I was smaller and by moving sideways I worked past the blocked doorway into the courtroom. By standing on one of the benches at the rear I could see all around the room over the heads of the people.

Mick stood in the front, up on the raised platform next to the judge's bench. He was cleaner, had his hair slicked back on the sides, and looked fresh in a pair of gray pants and an almost-white shirt rolled up at the sleeves.

He stood quietly, his elbow on the judge's bench, leaning sideways and watching with a small smile on his face—which still looked like it was made of hamburger. His eyes were still swollen almost shut and his lips were thicker than normal.

The crowd was jammed into every square foot of space, and near as I could see, not one of them was looking at Mick.

All around the walls, in two rows, one above the other, were drawings. Many of them were in the colored chalk—some I had seen him do, like the one of the small grave and drawings at the elevator, but most of them I had not seen before. Some were in pencil, some in charcoal, some just a few lines to show an idea, a few lines that showed everything, and many of them in more detail.

They were all of Bolton and for a second I just stared without seeing—there were so many. Dozens of them. And he had done them all in just two days and one night. One after the other, and they were all taped to the walls in the court-house, and it didn't seem possible that he could

125

have done it. Not in such a short time. But then I remembered that I had seen him do some of them in three, four minutes, his arm swooping with the chalk.

Then I started to look at the drawings, really look.

They were more than just drawings—they were pictures of Bolton, pictures of the inside of Bolton, pictures of everything.

"Look," somebody near me said, "look at Mrs. Langdon."

They meant the drawing. I saw it to the left of the bench on the wall. It was a chalk drawing in a partially lighted room, almost dim, and she was standing near a window looking back over her shoulder at the person looking at the picture.

She was nude.

Her hair was down and she was nude and it was one of those things you had to believe because of the things around it. There was the drawing of Jennings's dog, and there was Mrs. Langdon, and the drawing of the old car up on blocks, and there was Mrs. Langdon, and there were the sparrows at the elevator, and there was

Mrs. Langdon, and even if it weren't true, even if Mick hadn't seen Mrs. Langdon nude, it didn't matter.

The drawing made it true.

And more—more drawings of all the inside of the town. Drawings of the men in Lyle's Weak Beer Emporium that made them look coarse and ugly and thick-necked and drunk and red. Drawings of Mrs. Carlson holding a dollar in her hand and it was her, just exactly her, and she looked greedy and like she could hold on to the dollar forever and ever.

And me.

There was a drawing of me.

I was walking down the street with Python, holding on to his shoulder and the leg was there, the leg I didn't like to think about was there, and I could see it now, see it as others saw it, and I felt tears coming to my eyes. Not because I was sad or upset, but because I felt like I did when I saw the painting by Degas with the ballet dancers in it and I wanted to know them and they were gone.

And there was me and I wanted to know me,

to talk to me and ask me all about the leg and the dog, and I couldn't because it was me. I think in all the time of my life, in the long nights in the orphanage when we used to sneak into the bathroom and talk at night and bring cans of fruit cocktail and pretend to have picnics in there, in all the times of dreaming for somebody to come along and adopt me, in all the time of my life, I never saw me. Just me.

And there I was.

I started to choke up and saw that some others were crying and some—like Mrs. Langdon— were mad. She was standing in the middle of the crowded room staring, first at the drawing of her and then at Mick, who was not looking at her, and then back at the drawing and then to Mick. If she'd had a gun, I think he would have been dead.

Mrs. Carlson was the same. Off in a corner she was looking at the drawing of her holding a dollar. I thought it looked just as natural as life but she was so mad she was shaking. While I was looking at her she worked through the crowd to the wall and tore the drawing down and crumpled it and threw it on the floor.

It was as if everybody had been waiting just for that. People seemed to lean, then sway back, and then others came to the wall and did the same—tore the drawings down and crumpled them and stamped them on the floor. In moments most of the drawings were gone.

Mine was still there, and the old car and the Jennings dog and the little grave in the bushes and some of the elevator drawings showing the sparrows, but almost none with any people in them.

Things, I thought—they'll allow things, but they won't allow people.

Through all this Mick hadn't moved, stood leaning against the bench, and I hurt for him, thinking what they were doing to his art, but he was still smiling that small smile, and I realized that he knew it was going to happen all the time.

He had planned on it happening.

When they were done ripping and stamping, there was a moment when it was quiet—Mrs. Langdon staring at Mick, her chest heaving and her jaws so tight her back teeth must have turned to powder—and just then, just at that second, Mick stood away from the bench and said in a loud voice:

"Art."

Everybody froze, stared at him.

"Katherine Anne Porter once said art is what you find when the ruins are cleared away. I did this so that you could see, could feel, could know what this is all about—this monument. This art."

"Crap." Somebody said. "It's all crap."

Mick nodded. "That too, but that's part of it, isn't it? Art is everything. And this monument has to be that, has to be art, it has to hurt and make you weep and lift you into love at the same time."

"Tell everybody," Mrs. Langdon said, her voice sounding like breaking glass, "that you never saw me nude."

Mick stared at her, then sighed. "That doesn't matter, does it? That's how you would look if I *had* seen you without clothing, isn't it—looking over your shoulder near a window with the light on your hair and your shoulder turned just so to catch the light and the skin like cream, pure cream, and that sad look in your eyes because love, love is gone."

A strange thing happened then. Mick was talking but I was watching Mrs. Langdon and it all went out of her, all the mad went out of her. She seemed to wilt and sag back into the people standing around her, and the look changed, the way she was looking at Mick. It wasn't hate any longer, and not even sadness—it was more that she was drawn to him, maybe loved him. Right there in front of everybody she leaned down and picked up the drawing where she'd thrown it and smoothed it and tried to make it flat, all the while looking right at Mick, right into his eyes. I wished I had brought my tablet and pencils because I would have liked to draw that—draw the way she looked and the way Mick's picture was, crumpled, and how nobody else in the room seemed to be there for her, just Mick up next to the judge's bench. I wondered how come if it was *Mrs.* Langdon there was never talk of a husband, now or gone. But Mick wasn't looking at her.

"Art," Mick said, louder, "is all there is and this monument must be part of all of you to be true." He shrugged. "So, what is it, then? What do you want for your monument?"

The room exploded.

Some were still mad, although what Mrs. Langdon had done changed things and some of them had even picked up their drawings.

The noise was from ideas, but there were so many trying to talk at once it was just that, noise, and I couldn't tell what anybody was saying.

Mick held up his hand. "Just a minute." He went to the side of the room where there was a portable blackboard used to draw things for court. He carried the board to the front and took a piece of chalk from the rail.

"Now," he said, "one at a time."

"Let's do it with hands," Mrs. Langdon said, moving to the front of the room. "I'll call on you, each of you, and you can tell Mr. Strum what you want."

"Mick," Mick said. "Just Mick."

"Sorry," Mrs. Langdon said, looking at him, and I could swear she was blushing.

"And I'll call you Tru," he said. "That's how you signed your letter. It's a good name for someone with shoulders like cream."

Right there in front of the room it happened. You could see it. The thing between them was right there.

"Better than football, isn't it?" It was a low voice in my ear and I saw Fred standing there, leaning down. He and Emma had moved into the room when I wasn't looking. "I'm glad I didn't miss this."

"All right," Mrs. Langdon said. "Who's first?"

Hands shot up.

Mrs. Langdon raised her finger and pointed at somebody in back of me. It was Harley Pederson. He pretty much lived at Lyle's Weak Beer Emporium, had a head that looked like it had been screwed down into his shoulders, and was probably one of the men who beat Mick up.

"It should be a painting," he said, "of a soldier charging up a hill to save a blonde woman from avenging hordes"—he took a breath—"and it should be in glowing paint on black velvet."

I looked at Mick and he was smiling straight at me.

It was going to be a long night.

Sixteen

"HOLD IT," Mick held up his hands. It was close to midnight and people were tired and getting cranky, but the suggestions were still coming. Except that they weren't suggestions now so much as orders.

"I've listed the ones I thought I could do," he said. "And there are over a hundred. We could vote on each of them, but I think we would get one vote each a hundred times."

He rubbed the back of his neck and sat in the judge's chair to the rear of the bench. I read a story in the orphanage once about a leprechaun in Ireland and he looked like that—a leprechaun sitting in a judge's chair.

"How would it be if I made some suggestions and we voted on those—based on all your ideas, of course."

There was some muttering, and then somebody—I didn't see who—said, "What kind of suggestions?"

"I'm glad you asked." Mick stood and walked around to the front of the desk again. "We might be missing something, and I thought I would bring it up. The point is, sometimes monuments don't seem to be monuments but are, just the same."

"You're going to have to explain that," Harley said and I thought you'd have to explain just about anything to Harley.

"And I shall, I shall. All right, here's an example. Everybody here knows about the Battle of Waterloo, when Napoleon was defeated. After the battle women and children went around the battlefield with pliers pulling teeth from all the young men who had been killed—on both sides. Many people in France and England had bad teeth and needed false dentures, and they had no way to make false teeth in those days, so they used real teeth from dead people set in wood for false dentures."

"That's disgusting." This from Mrs. Carlson.

"No more than war, my dear—not a bit more disgusting than war. But the point I'm making is that those dentures—they called them Waterloo teeth in England, and only rich people could afford them—those false teeth were a kind of monument, weren't they? A kind of reverse, sick monument to all the young men killed in Waterloo. Every time one of those rich bas . . . people bit down on a piece of food they thought of the boy who had died."

Harley didn't get it. "You want us all to wear dentures?"

"No. I just want you to see that monuments can come from other places than just art. There's another story: During the Boer War in South Africa a platoon of forty-odd British soldiers were caught in a small valley by vicious crossfire. They were all killed and the bodies were left where they lay.

"They had just been issued their food, and each had been given a half a dozen peaches which the men kept in their knapsacks. As the bodies decomposed they became fertilizer and the peach pits took root, and now there is an orchard there, still today, of forty peach trees. It is said that the peaches from the orchard are the sweetest peaches in the world."

The room was silent, absolutely quiet. Even Harley kept his mouth shut.

Trees, I thought, all this time he was coming to this—he wants to make a monument with trees.

"It should be a place to think," Mick continued, "a place to remember the men who have died."

He went to the blackboard and began sketching in white chalk. "Here. Eighteen men have died from this area so here and here we plant trees, eighteen trees in two rows of nine in front of the courthouse on the lawn so that they make a shaded area and in the area we put seats, stone seats here and here and here so that people can come and sit in the quiet shade and think of what the trees represent."

He stopped, took a breath, waited.

All this time the room had been quiet and it was Harley who broke the silence. "There's a place there, by the courthouse, an empty place. What's that for?"

Mick pointed to the spot with the chalk. "For the future—it may be that you will want to plant more trees there."

Another quiet time, longer than before. I could hear the clock from all the way out in the hallway ticking.

"Could we"—a quiet, almost whispered man's voice cut the silence—"name them? Could we have a small plaque on each tree naming the one the tree is for?"

I turned and saw that it was Mr. Takern and remembered that he had a son killed in Vietnam.

"The name would mean so much," he said. "The names in Washington mean so much."

Mick nodded. "We can do anything you want."

Mrs. Takern stood suddenly from where she'd been sitting on a bench next to her husband and left the room, and I could see that she was crying, holding a hanky to her face. I wondered what her son's name had been and how he had died.

"Anything you want," Mick said again. "Do we need to vote?"

This time nobody made a sound and I knew that Mick had done it—had made the kind of monument he wanted to make for Bolton, the kind that Bolton truly wanted and just needed to be shown.

Trees.

Seventeen

AND OF COURSE nothing happened fast after the meeting. I wanted to be able to walk down the street the next day with Python and see the monument, see the trees and the names, but there were more things to do than just build the monument.

Mick had to figure a cost estimate for the trees and the stone seats and the labor, and when it was done he had to convince the town board that it was worth what it would cost, but that didn't take so very long. It seemed that in just a few days I saw a truckload of oak trees stopped in front of the courthouse. They were not large— each one ten or twelve feet—but they all looked healthy, and another truck had a kind of digger attached and in one day they had put all eighteen trees in the ground.

It was strange but when the men running the tree transplanter learned what the trees were for, they became quiet and worked without smiling. I wanted to help but Mick made Python and me sit next to the courthouse with our tablet and draw. I drew all the things I could see as fast as I could make my hands move with the pencil and still make it look right.

And Mrs. Langdon was there.

Except that she had changed and we didn't call her Mrs. Langdon anymore but Tru. She wore jeans and a sweatshirt and had all soft edges where she used to be hard and had a band holding her hair back. She helped Mick and always seemed to have a smudge of dirt on her cheek which she kept trying to wipe off with the back of her hand. I drew her, too, and once when it was a hot afternoon and she had been helping Mick clean dirt around a tree, he reached up and used his thumb to clean her cheek. She looked at him so that it seemed she had a light inside and I tried to draw that too. The light. And how it came from her eyes and Mick's eyes, except that I didn't do so well. But I tried, I tried to draw it all.

And there came a day when it was done.

"Done for now," Mick said. "It won't really be done until the trees are full grown—forty or fifty years—and then still won't be done until there are no more names or trees to put in. But done for now."

We were standing—Tru, Mick, Python, and I were standing by the end of the monument area. It was done and in some way looked like it had always been there. The last truck had brought in fresh sod and Mick and Tru and I—Mick finally let me stop drawing and help—cut and fit the sod around each tree and the stone benches in the middle so that no new dirt showed and it seemed to have always been.

"Tonight is the official showing," Tru said. "It is beautiful, Mick—what you've done. It's hard to look at it."

And it was—without crying. Next to each tree on a small stand stuck in the ground was a brass plaque with the name of a soldier and the date he had died. Later, when the trees were grown, each plaque would be fitted to a tree so that it would grow into the wood.

"Like the peaches, don't you see?" Mick had explained to us. "So that they are truly part of the wood and will live because the tree lives."

But it was not possible to look down the row of trees and see the names and not cry. It was in the same way as the Degas painting made me cry. They were all gone and I would never know them, and their lives did not go where they were supposed to go, but ended. Just ended.

"Tonight people will come and see what you have done," Tru said. "Are you proud?"

Mick looked at her and something passed between them that I did not understand, some knowing thing. He shook his head. "No. Not this kind of art. Any pride for me came when my art stirred up the hornet's nest in the courthouse that night—when I found you, found Tru, Mrs. Langdon. If it takes killing eighteen young men to get a piece of sculpture, you cannot be proud, can you?"

I knew then. I don't know how I knew, but I knew. "You're not going to be here tonight, are you?"

"Didn't I tell you she was cunning?" Mick said to Tru. "And isn't she?"

"You're going to leave."

"And I'm going with him," Tru said.

"It was always going to happen," Mick said. "I was always going to leave, wasn't I? And she was always coming with me. It's just that now it's time."

"But the monument . . ."

"It's not mine. It belongs to the eighteen men and to Bolton. There is other work to do now." He smiled. "Somewhere there is a place about to be overrun by paintings of Jesus and Elvis on black velvet, about to be swamped by ghastly

145

pictures of blondes with large breasts being saved by avenging heroes or gushy pictures of little girls and boys with large eyes."

"And only you can save them," I said, and as sad as I felt, I couldn't help smiling.

"There it is, isn't it?" He looked around at the town. "The Lone Artist rides again."

"And Tonto," Mrs. Langdon—Tru—said. "Let's not forget Tonto."

"Not a bit of it," he said. "One can never forget Tonto." He looked at me and was serious—or as serious as I'd ever seen him. "You will note what happens tonight, won't you? And draw it, catch it, and we will send a card from . . . where was that, my dear?" He looked at Tru.

"Westfalia," she said. "Westfalia, Texas—they want a statue in front of their new mall."

"Ahh, yes. Texas. We will send you a card from there and I wish a full report on the reaction."

"I'll do it."

"Then there is nothing else, is there?"

And I thought, *Oh, yes, oh dear God, yes, there are a thousand things to know and I want* to talk to you and listen to you but nothing came out, not a word. They climbed into the station wagon which I saw now was full of cardboard boxes, and it started with smoke and noise and drove away, turned a corner, and was gone.

Gone.

And I should have been sad and maybe I was, a little, because I knew there were tears on my cheeks and I was pulling and twisting kind of hard at Python's hair, but I was smiling because I couldn't help thinking:

God help Westfalia, Texas.

Dear Tru and Mick:

I'm sorry to hear you had to spend the night in jail, Mick, but you shouldn't have said that to the wife of the sheriff of Westfalia. You also shouldn't have written what you said to her on a postcard. I'm sure there are laws against it. But isn't it lucky that Tru was there to get you out and get the sculpture going?

You wanted a report on how it went here.

It was the strangest thing I've ever seen. There never was what you'd call a crowd of people and almost nobody talked. People kind of came all evening and walked down through the trees and nodded and smiled and seemed to be very polite, but when they looked down and saw the names on the plaques, even though some of them had been here before, you could tell it made them want to cry.

Even Harley was quiet and looked choked up. I stayed off to the side all evening until close to midnight, drawing. When it was too dark to draw I tried to memorize pictures that I could draw later.

I think everybody liked the monument, if like is the right word, and by midnight everybody was gone except for one person.

Mr. Takern had brought a little canvas folding stool, and he put it next to the tree with his son's name and sat there until after midnight. He didn't talk or anything, just sat, and once in a while he would reach over and pet the side of the tree, the bark, and I couldn't watch it after a while, but maybe after a long time I will be able to draw it.

I guess that's what makes an artist, isn't it?

Send me any new addresses you get, and I will report on any new developments with the monument.

Love,
Rachael

P.S. — I know — draw. I will.

Of *The Monument,* Gary Paulsen writes:

Ten or more years ago I read that Katherine Anne Porter once said, "Art is what we find when the ruins are cleared away."

Since then this book has worked at me. I wanted to show art, show how it can shake and crumble thinking; how it can bring joy and sadness at the same time; how it can own and be owned, sweep through lives and change them— how the beauty of it, the singular, sensual, ripping, breath-stopping, wondrous, frightening beauty of it can grow from even that ultimate ruin of all ruins: the filth of war.